For the grandmothers: Olive, Hilda, Sally and Kitty
And for Timmy, the actual cat with the crumpled ear,
and for Snif, the real street dog who was a
pussycat at heart.

KT-224-216

A round of "up-paws" for Badger the Mystical Mutt

"Set to be the Top Dog of children's books ... a magical debut of a book."
Social Literary

"Kids' book takes world by storm."
The Scottish Sun

"A moving and joyful story which warmed the heart of this cynical old journalist."
That's Books

"First-time winner."
The Evening Times

"A toast-loving, magical hound, who has been winning fans in book shops, libraries and schools across Scotland."
The List

"A charming and very funny children's story."
Diana Cooper

"McNicol & Jackson have created a charming new book character; a toast-crunching hound named Badger."
Aye Write, Glasgow's Book Festival

"A truly magical story which has all the hallmarks of a future children's classic!"
Ursula James

Badger
the
Mystical Mutt

and the Crumpled Capers

ABERDEENSHIRE LIBRARIES

1969691

JF

THE LUNICORN PRESS
Glasgow
Text © Lyn McNicol and Laura Cameron Jackson 2012
Illustrations © Laura Cameron Jackson 2012
All rights reserved

The moral right of Lyn McNicol and Laura Cameron Jackson
to be identified as author and illustrator of this work has been
asserted.

All rights reserved. No part of this publication may be
reproduced, stored in a retrieval system, or transmitted, in any
form or by any means, electronic, mechanical, photocopying,
recording or otherwise, without the prior permission of The
Lunicorn Press.

First published 2012 by The Lunicorn Press
1

Printed by Martins the Printers, Berwick-upon-Tweed
Designed and typeset by Heather Macpherson at
Raspberry Creative Type
Set in 14.25 pt Gentium Book

British Library Cataloguing in Publication Data
A CIP catalogue record for this book is available from the British
Library

ISBN: 978-0-9569640-2-1

www.badgerthemysticalmutt.com
www.facebook.com/badgermutt
www.twitter.com/badgermutt

"A magical 21st-century narrative which will delight and inspire folk of all ages."
Alex Lewczuk, Southside Broadcasting

"The toast-crunching, spell-muffing Badger the Mystical Mutt is a delightful, madcap, magical character, who worms his way into your affections."
Maggie Woods, MotorBar

"This book had me laughing out loud many times. The writing of McNicol and Jackson is brilliant, inspirational, charming and just plain fun."
BFK Books

"This story was another hit. My son absolutely adores Badger the main character, but I think it's the plot which always leaves him wanting more. It is definitely a page-turner for young children."
Missing Sleep

"There are some underlying morality themes that should allow vigorous class discussions."
Lomax Allwood, The School Librarian

"Badger the Mystical Mutt is the coolest doggie around and, in his brilliant stories, he helps young kids understand their world and believe in themselves and their ambitions."
Vegetarian Living Magazine

Also by McNicol and Jackson

Badger the Mystical Mutt

Badger the Mystical Mutt and the Barking Boogie

Badger
the
Mystical Mutt
and the Crumpled Capers

Lunicorn

...raising your spirit

Chapter One

It was almost 300 fathoms of winter, and everything in Badger the Mystical Mutt's garden was a little bit crumpled.

The frozen leaves crumpled and scrunched under Badger's paws. His famous time-travelling contraption — the Wim-Wim for a Wowser to wind up the weather on a wet day — had a crumpled crank shaft. And Badger's pal, Timmy (the cat with the crumpled ear) was in a spot of bother.

Timmy was keen to join the local gang of misfit mutts which was now led by Snif, a street dog with a fearsome reputation. But no cat had ever been allowed to join the notorious all-dog gang ... and Timmy wasn't just *any* cat.

He was a cat with an unusually crumpled ear. He was also a cat who was famous for all the wrong reasons. For Timmy could clear the lane instantly with his enormous snot-covering sneezes.

Badger had tried and failed to persuade him that joining Snif's gang was "Not a Good Idea", but Timmy would not listen.

So, Badger had to get his Wim-Wim working again. Then he could take Timmy to the Crystal Cave and find a way to get him into the gang. He looked fondly at the Wim-Wim's tilting feet and wilting brolly.

Badger munched on some toast, scratched his head and pulled his red-spotted neckerchief closer around his neck. The freezing temperature was nipping at his nose and, with every munch, he could see his breath in the air.

It was so cold that even the duck pond had completely frozen over, and all the

ducks had scarpered to somewhere cosier.
He peered at the Wim-Wim's fuel tank, and
wondered if its fuel had frozen too.

He joogled the contraption from side to
side and heard a sloshing sound.

"Hmmm" he thought "At least *all* of the
fuel hasn't turned to ice, but it still doesn't
sound like there's much in there."

The Wim-Wim ran on Haboba Juice,
a very strange brew indeed.
Badger reached into
the shed and pulled out
a can. He looked at the
label to check if any of
the ingredients were
likely to freeze. He
read out the list, item
by item, and pondered.

"Chilli peppers?
They're not chilly,
they're hot, so they should be okay." He
took another bite of toast.

"Carrot mush? Well, that does have some
water in it, but still ..." He scratched his chin.

"Syrup of figs? Now that should keep the Wim-Wim running, and is surely far too gooey to freeze?

"And last but by no means least, the burp of a big-footed Yeti. That's a tricky one." Badger swallowed his last morsel of toast and burped. "Oops, pardon me," he chuckled.

He filled up the Wim-Wim's fuel tank, shoogled it a bit more and waited. But nothing happened. It didn't clatter. It didn't clang. It didn't pant or putter. Instead, the rotor blades on top wilted a little bit more.

Badger frowned

"Okay, I'm worried now. It isn't like the Wim-Wim at all. This calls for one of my Badgical-Magical spells."

He rubbed his paws together then rummaged in his favourite plant pot for the perfect potion. He pulled out some nuts and bolts, tools and soap, and a pile of pongy old cloths, then set them out alongside the tin can of Haboba Juice and closed his eyes.

Sparkles of light appeared around him as he uttered the magic words.

"Monkey wrench and soapy cloths,
Spanners and sparkles, and juice that froths.
Make the Wim-Wim stop its tilting,
and save its rotor blades from wilting."

Badger opened his eyes and stood back feeling very pleased with himself.

The Wim-Wim spluttered and stuttered,

and glowed faintly. Badger held his breath
and hoped.

But then, the Wim-Wim faded into silence
again.

"Once more," he sighed. "And this time,
with Badgical-Magical gusto."

"*Monkey wrench and soapy cloths,*

Spanners and sparkles, and juice that froths. "

Badger shook his paws and shimmied his bottom. He scrunched his eyes shut.

"Make the Wim-Wim stop its tilting ..."

He whispered the last line with a determined spirit.

"...and save its rotor blades from wilting."

Badger opened one eye and saw the Wim-Wim's weather vane whirr weakly.

"Come on!" he urged. *"Please* get better."

The bottom of the Wim-Wim chugged and chuttered, and its rotor bearings rattled with the vibration.

Badger hopped from paw to paw, swishing his tail.

"I've done it, I've done it, I've done it! My spell worked. Wooftastic! Wait till I tell Timmy."

As Badger was busy dancing around his garden in delight, the Wim-Wim dwindled, the whirring weakened, the rotor bearings rattled no more, and the weather vane wobbled to a stop.

"Oh no, without my trusty Wim-Wim, I

can't help Timmy."

Badger put his head in his paws.

Meanwhile, at the far end of the lane, Timmy, the snotty-nosed cat with the crumpled ear, was facing his own challenge.

Chapter Two

The gang had Timmy pinned up against the fence. Pogo Paws held Timmy's left paw while Pickle gripped his right. Lennie held Timmy's legs tight. Snif stood in front of him smugly.

"So, you think *you* — a cat — can join our gang of *dogs*? Why would a sneezy cat with a crumpled ear want to do *that?*" sneered Snif.

Timmy puffed out his chest. "Because I'm every bit as good as you, and I don't see why not."

He tried to wriggle free. Pogo Paws and Pickle held on tighter, but Lennie, who was busy daydreaming, lost his grasp.

"Oh no! I'm in charge of legs. Don't move!" shouted Lennie nervously.

"Get a grip, Lennie," snarled Snif.

"I don't know why I've been given *two*

legs, when Pogo Paws and Pickle have only got one paw each," he moaned.

"Zip it, Lennie!" sighed Snif.

"So, Timmy," continued the gang leader, "isn't there a mob of manky moggies like yourself that you could be hanging around with?"

"They probably won't let him in with that crumpled ear," barked Pogo Paws.

"He's not exactly pretty, is he?" scoffed Pickle.

"I don't think he looks too bad," said Lennie.

"Zip it, Lennie!" shouted the gang altogether.

Lennie's shoulders hunched and he held on tightly to Timmy's legs.

"Now, if you really want to join, we need to see if you're up to being a member of our gang, so you need to pass our test," said Snif.

"Okay," said Timmy eagerly. "What do I need to do?"

"Can I let go yet? My paws are sore," asked Lennie.

Snif ignored Lennie and turned away from Timmy and the gang. He thought for a moment, then spun round.

"Got it! Right, we'd like to do some trampolining. So your mission, should you wish to accept it, is to find us a tyre ... a *big* tyre ... a *really* big tyre ... and bring it back to us here, before dark."

"How on earth can I carry a great big tyre?" asked Timmy.

"Find a way!" snarled Snif.

Timmy struggled to get free from the vice-like grip of Pogo Paws, Pickle and a slightly slumped Lennie. Suddenly, he felt a tickling in his nose.

"Uh oh," he winced. "I can feel a sneeze coming. Aaah, aah, aah ..."

Pogo Paws and Pickle looked up in

horror. Lennie put his paws
over his head.

"Aaaah, aaah,
aaah ..."

Snif ducked.

"Aaaaah, aaaah,
aaaah ..."

The gang waited for
the final explosion.

"Choooooooooooooooooooooo
ooooooo!"

"Yuk!" yelled the snot-covered

gang, as they ran away in disgust.

Timmy slid down the fence, shook

himself and headed for Badger the Mystical Mutt's garden.

"Badger!" shouted Timmy excitedly. "I can do it. I can join the gang."

"Wow" said Badger. "How did you manage that? I've been worrying about getting the Wim-Wim to work, so that I could take you to the Crystal Cave, and we could work out a plan. And now, it's all sorted. Toastastic!"

"Ah!" said Timmy. "There's just one *tiny* thing I have to do, and then I can join."

"Oh?" said Badger, raising his eyebrow. "I have a feeling I'm not going to like this."

"It's easy-peasy lemon squeezy," said Timmy. "I've just got to find a really big tyre, and carry it back to them."

"Hmmm," said Badger frowning. "The last time I checked, tyre-carrying wasn't in my *Book of Normal Cat Activities.* How exactly will you transport it with your small paws and sharp claws?"

"Erm ... I haven't thought that far ahead yet," said Timmy, stroking his whiskers.

"That task is impossible for a cat. Snif's being cruel. It looks like we definitely need the Wim-Wim," said Badger. "But I don't really understand why you want to join a gang like that anyway."

"What's wrong with the Wim-Wim?" asked Timmy, ignoring Badger's question. "Maybe I can take a look?"

"Please do," said Badger hopefully.

Timmy walked around the Wim-Wim and examined it carefully.

"I'm just going to tickle its reverse check plunger and see if its orbital gears are greasy enough," said Timmy seriously.

"I never knew you were skilled in mechanics, Timmy."

"I'm not. But I do have six *and a half* senses, Badger. I am a cat after all."

Timmy tapped his paw and poked his claw into the body of

the Wim-Wim. Suddenly, its rotor blades started to whirr and its weather vane whirled.

Badger smiled expectantly.

Then everything flopped again.

"When did the Wim-Wim have its last service, Badger?" asked Timmy.

"Um ... er ... never. The Wim-Wim has always worked," replied Badger.

"Well then, it's as I thought," said Timmy knowingly. "The freezing temperature has affected its orbital gears. The Wim-Wim needs a full service with a proper Wim-Wim mechanic. It's time for its Magical Orbital Transplant."

"It's MOT? But that's not due until Jupiter eclipses Pluto."

"It's not that simple," said Timmy. "It needs to be done now. Really, Badger, if you don't get it sorted, you may have to scrap the Wim-Wim."

Badger gasped. The thought of losing his Wim-Wim filled him with sadness and fear. Without it, he couldn't visit the Enchanted

Forest and the Crystal Cave, and couldn't be as Badgical Magical as he wanted to be.

He rubbed his neckerchief in anguish.

Suddenly, sparkles of light appeared around him, as his neckerchief unfurled from his neck and pointed upwards in the shape of a giant capital "C".

"Captain Bravebark!" shouted Badger in glee. "Of course, I forgot. Thank you, 'Chief."

Timmy looked at the neckerchief floating in mid-air and asked, "Who on earth is Captain Bravebark? How do you know him? How can he help us? And where is he?"

"Captain Bravebark lives in the Ring of Brodgar. A *very* Badgical-Magical place, Timmy. He also happens to be one of my relatives and a very clever one too. He's qualified in MOTs, and has the only other time-travelling machine in the universe which stops off at the Crystal Cave."

"Wow!" said Timmy. "I've heard about the Crystal Cave."

Badger continued: "I haven't seen him for many a dog year, but he always helps me when I need him and, right now, I need to send him a p-mail about using the Tangerine Piano as soon as possible."

"A tangerine what?" asked Timmy, more than a little impressed.

"Piano," said Badger casually, "with an ivory staircase."

"Blimey!" said Timmy, starting to sniffle and snuffle.

"Uh oh! I'm off before you start sneezing again," said Badger, as he disappeared through the crack in the fence, to send the all important p-mail to Captain Bravebark.

Still sniffing, Timmy followed him into the lane and bumped immediately into the gang. At the same time, he sneezed, showering the gang once again with snot.

"Yuk! That's disgusting! We need a snot shield with you around," snarled Pickle, wiping herself down.

"Not found your tyre yet?" taunted Snif.

"Hope it doesn't *tire* you out looking for the tyre, Timmy," jeered Pogo Paws.

Timmy wiped his nose, shrugged and slunk away. His six and a half senses started to twitch and his whiskers prickled. He trotted up a hill and into a nearby field, where he spotted one of the Big Folk in winter wellies changing a huge tractor tyre.

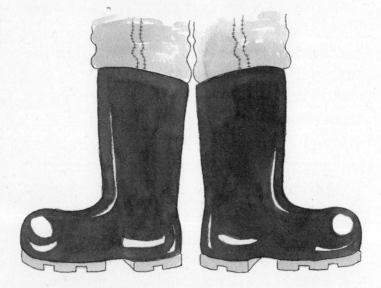

"Aha!" thought Timmy. "Now's my chance."

Timmy tiptocd up to the tractor and hid behind the toolbox.

He peeked over the top of the tools and watched.

The farmer lifted the old tyre from the wheel and leaned it against the tractor. Timmy stole closer, crept under the engine and waited. When he saw the Big Folk wellies walk away, he leapt inside the discarded tyre.

But the tyre wobbled and Timmy felt it move. Everything started to look a bit topsy-turvy.

"Oi!" shouted the Big Folk Farmer, as the wheel rolled down the hill, with Timmy clinging on with all his might.

"Whoa!" yelled Timmy. "This is making me dizzy."

The tyre raced towards the duck pond, clipped a tree trunk, juddered and changed direction, heading for the bins at the top of the lane.

"Crikey!" he shouted, as the tyre bounced off the bins sending the lids clattering and rolling alongside him.

The wheel gathered more and more speed as Timmy revolved towards the lane where the gang were having their afternoon nap.

Pickle was the first to awaken with the rumble. She looked up and saw the tyre hurtling towards them. She pulled Pogo Paws quickly out of the way. Lennie awoke with a start and grabbed onto Pogo Paws' disappearing tail.

But Snif was too late to move as the cumbersome tyre trundled on.

Chapter Three

The tyre bounced off the fence at the far end of the lane, swivelled and landed with an almighty thud.

The gang emerged from their hiding places to see Timmy fall out of the tyre, looking shaky and dazed.

Timmy stood up unsteadily and shouted "Ta da!" with his paws held out. "I did it! Here's your tyre. Now can I join the gang, please?"

The gang was speechless.

"Er ... where's Snif?" asked Timmy.

The gang pointed nervously behind Timmy.

A white tail was sticking out from underneath the heavy tyre, and Timmy heard a muffled whimpering sound.

A crumpled shape staggered out. It was

Snif, with a flattened nose, squashed paws and trampled ears.

"So, you think you're a smarty-pants, do you?" spat Snif, as three teeth tumbled out of his mouth.

The gang closed in behind their leader. Timmy cowered.

"Did you think that was funny?"

Timmy cowered some more. The gang moved forward.

"Has the cat got your tongue, Timmy? Speak to me! Explain!" bellowed Snif, spitting out another tooth.

"I couldn't see. I was moving so fast, I didn't know you were there. I'm really sorry. I didn't mean it. I thought you wanted a tyre, so I brought you a tyre," said Timmy apologetically.

Snif shook himself vigorously and turned to his gang.

"Right, that was small fry compared to the next of Timmy's tasks."

"Is there another task?" asked Lennie "What is it?"

"Zip it, Lennie! I'm thinking," snarled Snif.

Timmy's teeth chattered. He smiled awkwardly at Lennie and said, "It's just the cold weather. It's not because I'm frightened or anything."

"Right, Crumpled Lug, here's one for you. Dogs do tricks. Cats don't. So your task is to fetch us a stick thrown by one of the Big Folk and bring it here, within the hour."

Snif dusted himself down and turned on his heels, followed quickly by his gang.

Timmy scratched his head. "Could be tricky," he thought. "I think I need some Badgical-Magical help with this one."

When Timmy reached Badger's garden he smelled burning.

He peered through the crack in the fence and saw Badger busy making toast over a tiny crackling fire.

"I can't get my butter to soften in this cold air, and I can't put it too near the fire, or it will just go runny," muttered Badger.

"What to do, what to do?"

He turned around to see Timmy at the end of the garden.

"Couldn't you do a butter-melt spell?"

suggested Timmy.

"Good idea, Timmy, except I tried that once before and it went a bit awry. I believe the Big Folk call it *global warming*."

"Oops!" said Timmy with a smile.

"So, how did it go with the tyre task? Are you now a member of the gang?"

"Not quite. It's a bit of a sore subject actually ... particularly for Snif."

"Why do you want to be part of that gang anyway, Timmy? Cats and dogs don't generally get on."

"But why not?" asked Timmy innocently. "We all live on the same lane."

"Something to do with a misunderstanding hundreds of years ago about tail-wagging, I believe," said Badger. "Plus, I don't think there's ever been a cat in Snif's gang."

"Why?" asked Timmy.

"Simple really. When *you* wag your tail as a cat, it means you're a bit annoyed and you might want to fight. When *we* wag our tail as dogs, it means we like you and we're happy.

You can see how it could get confusing between us."

"Okay, I can see that. But why has Snif got such a problem with *me*?" asked Timmy.

"Well, maybe Snif's had a mishap with cats before. We just don't know what's happened to him in the past."

Timmy furrowed his brow.

"Anyway," said Badger brightly, "I have a special treat for you."

"For me? It's not even my birthday," said Timmy, as his eyes widened.

"Well, I think you did well completing the task they set you, even if *they* don't. It seemed impossible, yet you managed to do it. So, I would like to award you with one of my rarely awarded Badger badges."

Badger produced a shiny silver round badge from his plant pot and pinned it on Timmy's collar.

Timmy stood tall and looked proudly down at his shining badge.

"Thank you, Badger. I will treasure this forever, and that's given me the will to go and do the next task."

"What *next* task? You mean there's another one?" Badger sighed. "It's an easy one this time. Don't worry."

Timmy turned and walked confidently through the crack in the fence, out of the lane and up the hill into the nearby field.

There, the same Big Folk farmer, who had been changing the tyre on the tractor, was now loading logs onto the back of a trailer.

"Aha!" thought Timmy. "There are some sticks ... really, really big sticks."

As the Big Folk farmer jumped into the tractor and started up the engine, one large log rolled off the back and fell heavily to the ground.

Timmy spotted his chance and jumped on top. He rocked it backwards and forwards until it began to roll.

And roll ...

"Rock'n'roll!" shouted Timmy gleefully,
running on top as the log rolled along.

"Wooohooooooo!" he squealed as it got
faster and faster.

The log sped down the hill, but it was
heading straight for the gang.

Chapter Four

As the log trundled on, Timmy saw a Big Folk cycle towards him.

"Oh no!" he panicked, just as the cyclist lifted his head and saw the huge log in his path. He swerved just in time and landed in a ditch.

"Phew, that was close!" Timmy breathed a sigh of relief. But his worries were not over yet as the log crunched through the frozen puddles towards the fence at the far end of the lane, gathering even more speed.

The gang, who were rummaging amongst the wheelie bins for scraps of food, heard the sound of ice cracking and a thundering rumble. Pogo Paws looked up and saw the massive log, with Timmy on top, coming closer and closer. He bounced quickly out of the way, yelling to Pickle to do the same.

Lennie, who had his nose stuck in a half-empty tin of Buddy Bites, heard the shouting and, just in time, jumped into the bin.

Snif was nowhere to be seen.

The log hit the fence with full force and came to an abrupt standstill.

All was quiet. Timmy looked around him.

One by one, the gang emerged from cover to see Timmy leap off the log proudly.

"Ta da!" said Timmy with his paws held out. "I did it! Here's your stick. Now, can I join the gang, please?"

The gang was speechless.

"Er ... where's Snif?" asked Timmy.

The gang pointed nervously to the massive log behind Timmy.

A clump of white fur was sticking out from underneath. In the silence, he heard a long low groan.

The log shifted slightly as two weary paws appeared over the top. Snif sprackled out from underneath and hauled himself upright.

Timmy cowered.

The gang glowered.

Snif glared.

Catching his breath, Snif yelled at Timmy: "So, is this your idea of a stick? Is this some kind of joke?"

"I couldn't see you. I didn't know you were there. I'm really sorry. I didn't mean it. I thought you wanted a stick, so I brought you a stick," cried Timmy.

Snif pulled some splinters from his paws and brushed himself down. The gang rushed to help him tidy his scruffy fur.

"Right!" yelled Snif. "This stops now. You're trying to make a fool of me."

"No, I'm not," said Timmy defensively.

"Okay, I have one final task for you. And if you don't manage it without some sort of tomcat-foolery, then you can forget *ever* joining my gang."

"Oh, goody! How about *Mission Impossible?*" suggested Pogo Paws bouncing up and down.

"Yes, let's make it a *really* tough one, boss," snarled Pickle.

"What *is* the task then?" asked Lennie.

"Zip it, Lennie!" said Snif, who was still trying to figure out a challenge big enough for the irritating moggie.

Without warning, Timmy sneezed his biggest sneeze yet, and saturated the gang.

Pickle looked at Lennie and pointed to her umbrella.

"See? That's a snot shield, Lennie. I was thinking ahead."

As the gang wiped themselves down, Timmy said:

"I know why you're doing this, Snif."

"Doing *what?*" Snif huffed.

"Setting me impossible challenges; tasks you think I can't do, so that I can never join your gang. Badger the Mystical Mutt said it's all a misunderstanding."

"Badger the Mystical Mutt said *what?*" spat Snif viciously.

"He just explained why you don't want me in your gang. I'm a cat. It's as simple as that. And cats and dogs aren't supposed to get on together."

"Correct, Timmy! And by the way, you probably know this, but cats don't like water much either."

Snif booted a nearby garden tap with his paw and after a few spurtles and gurtles, a hosepipe sprang into life, releasing fierce, icy jets of water.

"Time for a shower, Timmy! Get him, gang!" yelled Snif.

Pogo Paws and Pickle sprang forwards and grabbed

Timmy's front paws. Snif nodded to Lennie to hold down his back legs.

Snif stood cruelly over the little cat and fired the coldest spray of water over him.

Snif cackled. Pogo Paws and Pickle sniggered, Lennie quivered and Timmy cried out.

"It's f-r-e-e-z-i-n-g. Please stop!"

But Snif would not stop.

Chapter Five

Back in his garden, Badger was staring hard at a pile of breadcrumbs that had been left out for the birds, thinking of a spell which could turn them into toast when, suddenly, screams pierced the icy air, followed by spine-chilling cat calls and screeches.

"That's Timmy," panicked Badger. "Uh oh, I need to go."

He sped through the crack in the fence and raced down the lane.

There, at the far end, he saw Timmy pinned to the ground by Pogo Paws, Pickle and Lennie, while Snif stood over him, firing water from a hosepipe.

"Oi!" shouted Badger. "Leave him alone. Let him go!"

The gang looked up, startled. Snif swirled and pointed the nozzle at Badger.

"Oh, it's the meddling mutt. Here, have some of this," he snarled.

Badger gasped as the icy cold water drenched him.

"Stop, stop, stop!" he pleaded. "Too cold."

"Oh, I'm *sorry*! I thought you wanted to join in the fun. After all, you're so clever at telling Timmy why he'll never be able to

join the gang," said Snif.

Timmy shivered. Pogo Paws tightened his grip, Pickle sniggered and Lennie asked, "Can I let go yet? I'm freezing."

Snif looked over his shoulder at Lennie and sighed.

Badger stood dripping. His neckerchief was soaked through.

"Maybe we need to hang you both out to dry. Get them, gang," ordered Snif.

Pickle and Pogo Paws let go of Timmy, ran to Badger and marched him into the nearest garden where a whirligig stood. Snif caught Timmy by the scruff of the neck and followed, with Lennie trailing behind.

"Now, let's get you pegged up," said Snif, as the gang hoisted them both up on to the whirligig.

Pogo Paws, with four pegs in his teeth, bounced up and pegged them to the line.

"Goodbye, boys," jeered Snif and the rest of the gang, as they ran off, leaving Badger and Timmy dangling.

Badger looked at Timmy. Timmy looked

at Badger.

"Any Badgical-Magical spells to get us out of this one?" Timmy asked hopefully.

"Erm, I might just have an unpegging spell that could work ... if I can remember the words," said Badger.

"Get thinking then, and fast. Otherwise

we're going to become icicles."

Badger closed his eyes and wrinkled his nose. Soon sparkles of light appeared around him. He uttered the spell:

"Peggie Weggie Whirligiggle,
Free your grip so we can wriggle.
Get us dry and spin us round,
then our paws can touch the ground."

Slowly, the whirligig began to move. It started to spin and whirl and twirl, getting faster and faster. Soon, it was revolving like a tornado. Badger and Timmy squealed.

"Wheeeeeeeeeeeeeeeeeeeeeeeee!" shouted Timmy.

"Woohoooooooooooooo!" yelled Badger, as they both wheeched through the icy breeze.

Then, without warning, the pegs opened and Badger and Timmy were flung to the ground mid-spin.

They stood up shakily and tried to walk.

They swayed and staggered, wibbled and wobbled and bumped into each other clumsily.

"Wow!" said Badger.

"I feel a bit sick actually," grimaced Timmy.

"Right," said Badger. "Let's get back to base and figure out what to do next."

They trotted, a little unsteadily, back to Badger's garden.

There, Badger picked up a p-mail from Captain Bravebark. The Tangerine Piano was tinkling and the ivory staircase was ready. It was time to fly to the Ring of Brodgar.

Chapter Six

Captain Bravebark had also sent his special spell to despatch Badger's trusty Wim-Wim for its repairs. Badger studied the spell and looked at Timmy hopefully.

"Okay, here goes."

He closed his eyes. Sparkles of light twinkled around the Wim-Wim as he uttered the magic words:

"With lullabies and dragonflies,
summon the trambulance of the skies.
Transport the Wim-Wim, with utmost care,
to the Ring of Brodgar. Carry it there!"

Just then they heard a loud *ding-ding* above them. Badger and Timmy looked up to see a massive white balloon with yellow stripes and a shiny silver bell, hovering just above the Wim-Wim. Ropes and loops appeared from beneath the balloon and wrapped themselves around the Wim-Wim.

Then, the Wim-Wim was lifted gently into the air and disappeared into the clouds.

Badger waved up to the sky.

"Okay Timmy. It's time to go. Are you ready?" said Badger.

"What just happened? Go where?" asked Timmy.

"That's the Wim-Wim off for its Magical Orbital Transplant, and that's where we are heading too; to the Ring of Brodgar, to jump aboard the Tangerine Piano and step up the ivory staircase to see my friend Nippy Nimbus. I haven't played it for many dog years, but don't let that worry you at all," smiled Badger.

"The Ring of Brodgar sounds like it's really far away from here," gulped Timmy.

"Nonsense! It's just a blink and a wink of flight. Hop on my back and hold tight."

Badger straightened his legs and shook his bottom until his tail whirred. Soon they were both flying high in the wintry sky.

As they climbed up and up, Timmy dared

to look down and saw the garden, the lane, the duck pond, the old oak tree and the fields become smaller and smaller. He shut his eyes and held on tighter, as Badger zoomed sharply to the left.

Timmy opened one eye, and saw a shimmering light in the distance. They seemed to be heading straight for it. Suddenly, Badger swooped and soared upwards.

"Hold on, Timmy, this is going to be colourful."

Timmy opened his other eye to find himself surrounded by a crimson glow. Badger glided forward into a glorious orange, which quickly swirled into a yellow and green and blue light.

"Wow!" shouted Timmy as they flew through an indigo haze. "What *is* this place?"

"This, my friend, is a rainbow, and we're just flying through it," replied Badger.

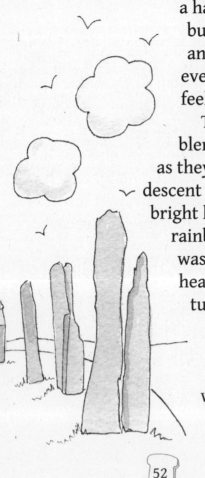

"Every one of my six and a half senses is buzzing already, and we're not even there yet. I feel amazing."

The indigo blended into violet as they began their descent through the bright light of the rainbow. Timmy was sure he could hear a faint tuneful jingle from below. Across the whispering wind, the sound burst into a cosmic symphony.

"I can see it. Look down, Timmy. There are the standing stones of the Ring of Brodgar. Don't they look magnificent?" yelled Badger.

"Groovy! This is the cat's whiskers!" Timmy shouted.

Badger flew downwards further still, until he saw a figure waving up at him.

"Who's that?" Timmy asked

"It's Captain Bravebark, bringing us in for landing."

Badger circled the standing stones before diving towards the grassy plain in the middle of the ring. He wobbled a bit and hit the ground with a bump.

"Still need to practise that landing," he muttered to himself.

Timmy caught his breath. Badger shook himself and Captain Bravebark scurried over to greet them."

"Good to see you, Badger. How long has it been?"

"Hundreds of dog years, Captain."

"Goodness, it seems much longer. Anyway, who's your friend?"

"This is Timmy, and I'm taking him to the Crystal Cave. Thank you so much for tuning the Tangerine Piano for me. Did my Wim-Wim arrive safely?" asked Badger hopefully.

Captain Bravebark twirled his moustache and said: "A few more tickles and turns Badger, and it will be ready. I'm just waiting on some new orbital gear bearings. You just can't get the parts these days."

"Thank you, Captain. You're the only Wim-Wim fixer left. I do appreciate it. Now, to business ... are there any new tunes we need to access the ivory staircase of the Tangerine Piano?"

"Let me think. You need to get straight on to Nippy Nimbus, don't you?" He scratched his head. "Why don't you try playing something by Beethoven? I think a Sonata should do it."

Badger walked over to the piano and sat down at the stool. He fluffed out his tail, straightened his neckerchief and shook out his paws. He lifted the lid and began to play the opening notes of Beethoven's *Moonlight Sonata.*

Timmy looked on in awe as the black and white keys started to lift at one end of the piano, and weave into the air. Soon, the rest of the keys had followed and a staircase formed, reaching up to the stars.

Timmy watched in wonder.

"See you when you get back," shouted Captain Bravebark, as Badger beckoned for Timmy to join him on the bottom step.

"C'mon, Timmy, we've got quite a climb ahead."

They leapt up the stairs two at a time.

After seventy-three-and-a-half flights, they were both huffing and puffing.

"Just a few more steps and we're there. I can see the top," said Badger encouragingly.

As they climbed the remaining

stairs, they heard strange mutterings and annoyed tuttings from above.

"That sounds like Nippy," sighed Badger.

"He doesn't seem very pleased to see us," said Timmy.

They popped their heads through the mist at the top of the ivory staircase to see cotton-wool fluffiness and a very grouchy cloud.

"Is there no escaping you, Badger the Mystical Mutt? And who is this you have with you this time?" bellowed Nippy Nimbus.

"Hi, Nippy. This is Timmy. Can you let us through, please?"

"Where's that pesky contraption you usually come in?"

"The Wim-Wim is getting its MOT. Captain Bravebark loaned me the Tangerine Piano and, I must say, it's always a delight to see you, Nippy," said Badger pleasantly.

"Okay, what's the password then?"

Badger scratched his chin and whispered to Timmy, "I hate this bit. He always tries to

catch me out.

"Okay," said Badger. "*Who let the dogs out?*"

"Nope!" smirked Nippy. "Try again."

Badger puffed and thought again. He looked at Timmy and tried, "*Cool for cats?*"

"Close ... but no. One last try."

Badger looked again at Timmy and grinned. "Right, last try. How about ... *What's new pussycat?*"

Nippy groaned. Badger had outwitted him again. "Be on your way then."

Reluctantly, Nippy let them through.

In front of them shone a dazzling light. Timmy shielded his eyes.

"Oh!" said Badger "We've been fast-tracked straight to the Crystal Cave."

And there, in front of them, stood Baby Unicorn.

"I heard the ivories tinkle and saw the rainbow shimmer, so I've been expecting you," winked the unicorn. "Step inside!"

Chapter Seven

Timmy followed Badger, who followed the *clip-clop* sound of Baby Unicorn's hooves as he led them both deep into the cave.

Timmy's eyes widened in wonder at the blaze of light inside. They walked under a dazzling crystal archway, past a stunning display of crystal rocks, and into a dimly lit chamber.

Timmy rubbed his eyes as they adjusted from the brightness. Everything was hushed.

"What happens now?" he whispered.

"Just watch," said Badger.

Baby Unicorn pointed his head towards the smooth rock on the cave wall. A beam of light whooshed out from the horn in the middle of his forehead. The cave wall flickered into motion like a movie screen.

There, Timmy saw an image of Snif as a much younger dog, chasing a burly tomcat across a field.

"That's Snif!" yelled Timmy excitedly.

"That's right. Watch and see what happens next," said Badger.

Back on the screen, Snif was catching up and, just as he was about to pounce, the cat shot upwards and bounded over a spiked railing.

Snif tried to leap the railing too, but he wasn't as nimble as the cat and couldn't clear it. He landed slap bang in the middle of the spike.

Timmy looked on in horror, as he watched Snif yelp and howl with the spike spearing his side. He was bleeding badly.

"Owww!" cried Timmy.

"It's okay, Timmy. Just watch. He'll be fine," reassured Badger.

The tomcat sat on the other side of the railing and smirked.

The picture flickered. Badger looked at Timmy and said softly: "I think we now understand why Snif hates cats. Let's see what happened next."

They peered back at the screen on the cave wall and saw the cat taunt Snif, before slinking off.

Just then, a Big Folk farmer drove up in his tractor, saw Snif and ran out to help.

The picture flickered again and showed Snif lying on his back with a huge red scar on his side.

"No wonder Snif doesn't like cats. That tomcat just left him there bleeding. It was horrible," said Timmy sadly.

"There's still more for us to watch, Timmy. Look," pointed Badger.

Back on the cave wall, another image appeared. This time, it was Timmy looking at his reflection in the duck pond. He was touching his crumpled ear and trying to flatten it out.

"That's me," murmured Timmy.

Badger said nothing. Then the image showed Timmy sneezing and wiping his nose with his paw as he tried to catch up with a clowder of cats, that was shouting at him to leave them alone.

"We don't want you with us, with that crumpled ear, scruffy coat and snotty snout. Crumpled Lug, Crumpled Lug, makes you look an ugly mug!"

"But I was born like this," Timmy whispered sadly. He walked back to the duck pond, his shoulders slumped and his head hung low.

The screen went blank. Baby Unicorn and Badger looked at Timmy, who suddenly seemed very, very lonely.

"So this is why you want to join the gang? Because the cats don't want you?" asked Badger kindly.

"I just want to have pals and fit in somewhere," said Timmy woefully.

"Look Timmy, Baby Unicorn could uncrumple your ear right now, and give you something to help your sneezes ... but I don't think that's the answer."

Timmy looked up hopefully. "Could he really?"

"Yes, but then you wouldn't be *Timmy*. That ear makes you who you are. It's part of you. The sneezes we can work on back home, with a herbal potion of nettles, ginger and saffron, and a lotion of parsley, chamomile and basil."

"Yuk!" said Timmy "I think I'd rather sneeze."

"Be proud of who you are and celebrate your crumpledness!"

Timmy wasn't entirely convinced, but nodded his agreement.

"Pet dander!" said Baby Unicorn.

"Dander what?" asked Timmy and Badger together.

"It's a bit like Big Folks' hay fever. That's what's causing your sneezing, Timmy. You're allergic to dogs."

"I can't be allergic to dogs, surely? I want to join their gang," said Timmy, flabbergasted.

"Goodness! So that's a *real* reason why cats and dogs can't be together?" asked Badger.

"It's very rare for cats to be allergic to

dogs and, as you well know, Badger, there's no such thing as problems … only solutions. And in this case, it's a simple course of papaya and pineapple."

"Aha! But they could be tricky to get in winter," said Badger.

"I'm sure you'll find a way, Badger," Baby Unicorn smiled.

"Okay," said Badger bowing. "Thank you, Baby Unicorn. So, now we know why Snif is horrible to you, perhaps we can help sort this out before a cat-astrophe occurs between you both."

Baby Unicorn bowed, and Badger led the way out of the cave where they all heard the distant tinkle of the ivory staircase.

Back in the lane, Snif was holding a meeting with Pogo Paws, Pickle and Lennie, to decide Timmy's last and ultimate challenge.

"It's got to be something that he won't *ever* manage," said Pickle.

"Yes, something mammoth, that even his

six and a half senses can't overcome," added Pogo Paws.

"What's the point of that?" said Lennie.

"Zip it, Lennie!" said Snif. He touched the jagged skin of the scar on his side and growled.

"This is payback time. It's time we showed those cats who's boss. *This* is for the whole of dogkind, everywhere."

At the Ring of Brodgar, Captain Bravebark was waiting by the Tangerine Piano. Badger and Timmy jumped off the last step of the ivory staircase and ran to greet him.

"Thanks, Captain," said Badger. "That was really helpful."

"Did you get what you needed?" he asked.

"That ... and more. Timmy had a trip he'll never forget," said Badger.

Timmy grinned widely.

"Righty-ho! Then you'd better get home. I'll send you a p-mail when the Wim-Wim's fixed, Badger," yelled Captain Bravebark.

But Badger was already high in the air with Timmy on his back.

Badger and Timmy landed in the garden with a thud.

"Goodness!" said Timmy. "Did that really just happen?"

"You'd better believe it," said Badger with a knowing wink. "So, maybe you understand Snif a bit better now?"

"Indeed I do. And now I know exactly what I need to do to get into the gang," said Timmy confidently, walking towards the crack in the fence.

Badger watched as Timmy left, wondering exactly what the cat was planning.

Chapter Eight

As Timmy stepped into the lane, he came face to face with Pogo Paws, Pickle, Lennie and Snif, who surrounded him.

Snif leaned in to Timmy's crumpled ear and, in a menacing whisper, said: "So, do you still want to join our gang, Snotty Nose?"

"Yes, but I understand why you don't like cats now," he answered bravely.

"It's not *all* cats. Just you," shouted Pogo Paws.

"Yes, it's only crumpled snivelling cats that we dislike," added Pickle.

"I think you're okay for a cat," said Lennie affectionately.

"Zip it, Lennie! It's not just him ... it's *all* cats. They're rotten to the core," spat Snif.

The gang looked at their leader, surprised

at just how completely anti-cat he was.

"I saw what happened to you before, with the cat, Snif," offered Timmy.

"What do you mean? Saw what?" sneered Snif.

"I saw you chasing that tomcat and getting caught on the railings."

Snif looked uneasy, turned to his gang and joked: "I have no idea what he's talking about. Maybe we should add 'daftness' to Timmy's list of freaky features."

"But I saw it. It was awful how the cat just left you on that spike. Can I see your scar?"

Instinctively, Snif held his paws to his side, as he felt the familiar itch of his scar, bringing back painful memories from years before. He shuddered.

"You told me you wrestled an escaped tiger to the ground, and that's how you got your scar," said Pickle, a bit puzzled.

Snif winced and shifted uncomfortably on his paws.

"And you told me that you were wounded when you tamed a bull, like a matador," said Pogo Paws, a little peeved.

"I thought you said you grappled a crocodile in the pond to save the ducks," added a disappointed Lennie.

"It was none of those," said Timmy. "It was just a cat."

Snif looked away in shame.

"Badger showed me," continued Timmy. "And thank goodness he did, because I want you to know, Snif, that all cats aren't like the one who left you bleeding there that day."

Snif turned round sharply and snorted in rage: "Badger? Why is he filling your head with this nonsense?"

"But it's *not* nonsense," pleaded Timmy.

"We'll soon see about that," barked Snif, as he raced off to find Badger.

"Oh no, what have I done?" worried Timmy.

In Badger's garden, all was not well. His secret stash of toast was looking very soggy. Badger's easy un-freezy spell was not working out as planned. He peered into the puddle in front of him, at the leftovers of his wonky spell. Suddenly, in the reflection, he spotted a shadow behind him. His neckerchief twitched in warning.

Badger spun around, to see Snif skulking at the bottom of his garden, looking like he was about to pounce.

Very quietly, Badger spoke to his red-spotted neckerchief: *"Show Koo Ray, Show Koo Ray, Show Koo Ray 'Chief, shield me quickly from this angry stray."*

Without hesitation, 'Chief flew off Badger's neck and headed straight for a nearby tree. Slicing the icicles off its branches in one swift motion, 'Chief fired them one by one into the frosty ground around Snif, encircling him in a cage of ice.

"Let me out, let me out, you meddling mutt," begged Snif.

The neckerchief flew back and wrapped itself snugly around Badger's neck.

"Thank you," said Badger, tapping 'Chief softly in appreciation. "Now," said Badger, walking around the circle of icicles which held Snif captive. "What has got you so angry, my friend?"

"Friend? Friend? You're no friend of mine," said Snif enraged. "Why did you tell Timmy about my scar, and how do *you* know about that anyway?"

"It doesn't matter how I know. What matters is that you believe that Timmy isn't like the cat that left you that day."

Snif started to get agitated again as he remembered the pain of the spike.

"Cats are all the same: cunning, sneaky and vicious," he spat.

"But it's the same for dogs, some would say. Most are really nice, but the odd one isn't," said Badger softly.

"At least when we wag our tails, it means we're happy and friendly. When a cat wags its tail, it's not that simple," said Snif.

"True. And that's maybe where this confusion comes from. Just a misunderstanding about tail-wagging."

Snif thought for a moment, then listened

as Badger continued. "There isn't a line drawn with dogs on one side and cats on the other. Yes, we *are* different, but we're all on the same side. We breathe the same air and we live under the same sky."

"But Timmy's even more different than most cats," said Snif.

"And that's another reason you should be less harsh towards him. He's struggling to fit in, especially with you lot calling him names and excluding him," said Badger.

"But that stuff that comes out of his nose is disgusting, and even some of the Big Folk don't want to pick him up with his crumpled ear."

"How would you feel if that happened to you?" asked Badger.

"Well, I don't do much rolling over for tummy rubs because of my scar," said Snif.

"Exactly!" said Badger. "So, think how Timmy feels when everyone can see his unusual ear? He can't hide it."

"I didn't think about it like that," said Snif thoughtfully.

"Anyway," added Badger, "you should be proud of your scar. You survived. It's part of you, and it's part of your history."

As the icicles around him began to melt,

Snif touched the wound on his side with new affection.

"He did manage the tasks you set him, against all the odds," said Badger.

"He certainly did, although I suffered as a result," smiled Snif, revealing his missing teeth.

"Imagine if you could turn Timmy's skills to your advantage and use them for the good of the gang."

"I suppose, but I can't see how the gang would ever accept a cat."

"You're the leader. Persuade them," said Badger. "Oh, look at that. You're free to go. Your cage has melted."

Snif stepped across the puddles of water surrounding him and left Badger's garden with his heart a little lighter.

Further up the lane, an almighty sneeze was rumbling along in the breeze. A very determined Timmy was on his way to see Snif.

Chapter Nine

"Snif, Snif!" shouted Timmy as he caught sight of the gang's leader further up the lane, "Wait, I've had an idea"

Snif stopped in his tracks as the little cat ran to catch him up.

"I've been thinking," said Timmy, "and I've come up with the task to end all tasks; a challenge that is bigger than anything you've set me yet."

"I've been thinking too, Timmy," said Snif gently.

Just then, the rest of the gang appeared and interrupted them.

"Well, did you sort out that Mystical Mutt then?" asked Pogo Paws

"Yes, did you show him who's boss?" said Pickle.

"Did he give you any of his secret toast

stash?" asked Lennie hopefully.

Pogo Paws and Pickle looked at Lennie in despair.

"Yes, I did see Badger," said Snif gruffly. "He won't be bothering me again."

The gang looked at Timmy, who was hopping from one paw to the other, desperate to share his idea.

"Timmy's got an idea for the final task," said Snif. "Come on then ... spill!"

"Okay, it's a tree task. Now don't worry, it doesn't involve rolling tree trunks down hills," said Timmy.

Snif winced.

"So, as it's winter, the old oak tree at the other end of the lane usually has mistletoe up on its highest branches about now."

Snif and the gang looked puzzled.

"Mistletoe is used to calm the jitters; something I think we could all do with,"

offered Timmy.

Lennie perked up and nodded enthusiastically

"Plus, cats don't generally like climbing too high, because when we do, we tend to get ... erm ... a bit stuck. So my challenge would be to overcome all that by scaling the tree and picking the mistletoe to bring back to the gang. What do you think?" smiled Timmy triumphantly.

The gang muttered amongst themselves, then Pogo Paws announced, "Okay, go on then. Let's see what you're made of. Maybe it'll be third time lucky."

"As long as *we* get to choose which branches we want the mistletoe from," added Pickle sniggering.

"Fine by me," agreed Timmy.

Pickle and Pogo Paws took Lennie aside for a hushed conflab and, seconds later, he dashed off in the direction of the tree.

As Snif and Timmy discussed the details of the task, Lennie was undertaking a challenge of his own. As instructed by Pickle and Pogo Paws, he'd unhooked the hosepipe from the garden tap and had dragged it to the old oak tree. He looked upwards and shielded his eyes from the winter sun. He couldn't figure out how he was supposed to throw the hosepipe over one of the really high branches.

Just as he was about to give it up as an impossible job, he was joined by Pickle and Pogo Paws.

"Haven't you got it sorted yet, Lennie? Quick! Snif and Timmy will be here soon," said Pickle.

"But there's no way I can reach that," whimpered Lennie.

"Leave it to me," said Pogo Paws, who had spied the tractor tyre from the first task nearby. "It just needs some bounce," he shouted, as he grabbed the hosepipe, jumped onto the tyre and sprang up into the air.

He looped the hosepipe easily over the branch and boinged back down.

"Right, catch both ends, Lennie, and hold

onto them. When we give you the nod, pull them down as hard as you can."

Lennie crept into position just as Snif and Timmy rounded the corner.

"Are you sure you want to do this?" Snif asked Timmy.

The gang looked at Snif in disbelief.

"Yes, and maybe then you'll let me join your gang?" said Timmy. Pogo Paws and Pickle tittered. Lennie sighed.

As Timmy sized up the old oak tree, Snif caught sight of Lennie out of the corner of his eye.

"What's *that?*" he whispered.

"A giant cat-a-pult, I think," said Lennie.

"Are you impressed, boss? We've rigged the tree," said Pickle smugly.

"One way or another, Timmy's going for a long-haul flight today," added Pogo Paws.

"But that's not fair," cried Snif. "He hasn't got a chance and, what's more, it's dangerous."

"Ooooh, sorry! We didn't think you actually *wanted* Timmy to succeed, and join our gang," said Pickle defensively.

"We thought we were doing really well," added Pogo Paws.

"And I just do what I'm told," said Lennie.

"Either way, it's not a fair fight," said Snif.

"Right, I'm ready," shouted Timmy cheerfully. "Pick your branch, gang!"

Pickle and Pogo Paws pointed up at the booby trapped branch and sniggered.

Timmy started to scale the tree's trunk

and was creeping carefully onto its lower branches. Pogo Paws and Pickle put their paws round the bottom and tried to shake the tree.

"I can't watch this," sighed Snif.

"Come on, Timmy. You can get higher than that," taunted Pickle.

"Maybe the fresh air up there will stop your sneezing," added Pogo Paws.

Just then, Timmy sneezed ... then sneezed again ... and then again. Pogo Paws and Pickle managed to dodge the fallout of snot. They looked over at Lennie who was holding the hosepipe, covered in a slimy green mess.

"Nice one, Timmy," shouted Pickle. "Now, see that branch up there to the left? There's a sprig of mistletoe *just* there which I think will be perfect."

"Yes, if you

can get *that* one," added Pogo Paws, "I'm sure Snif will let you join our gang." He looked over to his leader for approval but Snif just walked away.

He didn't want to see the brave, innocent little cat hurt himself; not in his name. "There's a big difference between bravery and bravado," he thought.

As Timmy crawled along the branch towards the sprig of mistletoe, Snif headed in a different direction altogether, towards the frozen duck pond.

"Badger was right," he thought. "This is all wrong."

Suddenly, Snif skidded and landed on his tummy. His snout was flat to the ground as he raced across the ice.

All Snif heard next was a crack as the ice below him broke. He yelped at the shock of the icy water on his body. He thrashed and gasped, flailing helplessly as the depths of winter sucked him under ... and under.

Then all was silent.

Chapter Ten

At the old oak tree, Timmy crept along the branch.

"Pull it tighter *now,* Lennie!" spat Pickle.

As Lennie pulled the hosepipe ends taut, the branch pointed downwards. Timmy lost his balance and slithered nose-first towards the mistletoe. He clung on bravely.

"Where's Snif?" shouted Pogo Paws.

"I don't know," said Pickle. "But he's missing the best bit."

"He left ages ago," called Lennie.

In Badger's garden, the Mystical Mutt was snoozing, but the commotion from the other end of the lane woke him with a start.

"This has got to be something involving Timmy," he thought. He straightened his legs, shimmied his bottom and flew off to investigate.

Still not good with landings, Badger arrived with a bump at the tree where the gang were gathered, right next to Lennie's makeshift catapult.

The surprise of Badger's sudden arrival startled Lennie who immediately let go of the hosepipe. The branch sprung upwards with an almighty ping and sent Timmy soaring into the sky at the same time as the

gang scarpered.

"Where did everyone go?" said Badger aloud, to the emptiness around him.

He sniffed the tree and picked up Timmy's scent, then saw the branch with the hosepipe hanging from it limply.

"Uh oh! I'm sensing that Timmy *has* been here. But where is he *now*? It's time to consult my all-seeing toast."

Timmy had landed slam-bang in the middle of the frozen duck pond. Luckily, he had fallen on a patch of thick ice. Sure-footed as ever, he picked himself up and, using his claws as crampons, made his way across the ice to where there was a large gaping hole.

His six and a half senses prickled. Something was very, very wrong. He peered into the blackness of the water, and was sure he could see a few bubbles.

"Oh no, surely not!" gasped Timmy, as he teetered over the edge and saw a shadow floating lifelessly just beneath the surface of the water.

The Mystical Mutt had just one remaining slice of precious toast hidden away in his garden. He pulled it out and examined it closely. Could the toast tell him the whereabouts of his friend Timmy?

"*Come on, Toast, show me the place where Timmy has gone. Please show his face!*"

At the duck pond, Timmy took a deep breath and plunged his paws into the icy water. He flinched as he touched Snif's wet fur.

"Snif! Snif!" he shouted, but the dog didn't respond.

Timmy had to act, and quickly. He undid his own collar and felt around for the old piece of rope around Snif's neck.

With one paw, he caught hold of the sodden rope and looped his collar around it. Then, he looked around for a sturdy branch to grab onto with his other paw, and pulled on the rope with all his might.

Slowly, the limp lump of fur came to the surface.

Timmy jumped back from the tree, still hanging on to his collar and edged forward to the hole in the ice. As he grabbed hold of Snif's shoulders, his own collar, with his prized Badger badge attached, fell into the depths below.

Inch by inch, he heaved Snif's heavy form out of the water and up onto the ice. He pushed and pushed until they were both clear of the danger and on the grassy verge.

Timmy listened at Snif's chest for a heartbeat.

Suddenly, a big dark shadow loomed over them. Timmy looked up to see Badger hovering above.

"I came as soon as I could," panted Badger. "The toast showed me where you were. Oh my goodness, what have you got here? Is that Snif?"

"Quick!" said Timmy "He needs a miracle and some of your Badgical-Magical healing."

Badger landed swiftly and, for once, without a thump. He took one look at Snif.

"Stand back," he said. "This is a job for 'Chief."

He tapped his neckerchief urgently and said, *"Show koo ray, show koo ray, show koo ray.*

Revitalise our friend, before he fades away."

'Chief flew immediately off Badger's neck and started billowing over Snif.

"That's the kiss of life," said Badger as sparkles of light twinkled around him. "I just hope we're not too late."

They both watched anxiously as 'Chief continued its mission to revive Snif.

After what seemed like an age, 'Chief finished its task and formed a blanket over Snif.

Badger and Timmy laid their heads against his fur and listened.

His heartbeat was weak and faint, but at last, Snif was breathing.

"Right," said Badger relieved. "Let's get you both back to my garden for some hot toast and blankets. Hop on."

'Chief wrapped himself around Snif to form a sling. Badger straightened his legs, wiggled his bottom and took off, pulling Timmy and Snif along below him.

When they arrived in the garden, Badger ran inside to his Big Folk's house and appeared moments later, carrying warm fluffy blankets and a pile of toast dripping with butter.

"Into the shed, both of you!" he ordered.

Inside, with their teeth chattering and their bodies shivering, they wrapped the blankets around them, and chomped on the toast hungrily.

Snif, who had come round a bit, thanked Timmy for his bravery, and Badger for his neckerchief.

"Timmy, where's your collar? And your Badger badge?" asked Badger.

Timmy shrugged his shoulders. "I had to use it to rescue Snif, and it fell into the hole in the ice. There wasn't any time to try and find it. I'm sorry, Badger."

"Don't worry, Timmy. I think you had more important things to think about," said Badger kindly.

Snif looked apologetically at Timmy and they all munched on some more toast.

"Oh!" said Badger in surprise, "Snif's ears have turned purple."

Snif raised a weary paw to touch them. "I can't feel them," he said. "They're numb. It's probably the cold."

"Don't rub them," warned Timmy, "otherwise you could end up with crumpled ears too."

"If I had even half of your courage, I'd be happy with a couple of crumpled ears," said Snif yawning. "It doesn't matter what you look like in order to shine. It's what's in your heart that matters."

And with that, Snif fell fast asleep.

"Oh dear!" said Badger. "I think Jack Frost has had a nip of Snif's ears. We're going to have to warm them up slowly to stop severe frostbite, otherwise he'll lose them."

As Snif slept soundly, Badger set to work. He tapped his neckerchief again and asked it to form a heated bandage around their friend's ears.

"'Chief, 'Chief, wrap up Snif's lugs. Keep them

warm and give them hugs."

Badger's neckerchief unfurled dutifully from his neck and wrapped itself around Snif's ears. As Timmy and Badger snuggled in for the night, only morning would tell whether Snif would be dog-eared and crumpled ... or not.

Chapter Eleven

The next morning, Snif woke first. He was groggy and thirsty and felt something on his head. He reached up and touched what seemed like a bandage around his ears. He quickly remembered the events of the day before.

Badger, who had been keeping a watchful eye on Snif throughout the night, said, "Let's take a look at your ears."

Snif grimaced as Badger and Timmy took an ear each and gently removed the neckerchief bandage, worried as to what they might see.

"The tips look fine," said Badger, unwrapping a little bit more.

"The fur seems soft enough," said Timmy.

"Uh oh!" said Badger. "This one looks a bit blue."

"And this one is covered in blisters," said Timmy.

"Can you feel that, Snif?" asked Badger, poking a paw into his ear.

"Ouch, yes!" yelped Snif.

"Well, that's a good sign. I think you'll be back to normal in a day or so. 'Chief has done an amazing job," sighed Badger in relief.

"Good work," he said to 'Chief as it shook itself out and wrapped back around the Mystical Mutt's neck.

"No crumpledness at all," joked Timmy.

"Now, 'Chief and I have to go and see about something very important. I'll leave you two here to have breakfast. There's still some toast left from last night, and there's water in that dish in the corner," said Badger.

Badger slipped through the crack in the fence and into the lane where he spotted Pogo Paws, Pickle and Lennie with their heads down.

They seemed to be on a trail and were

106

engrossed in following a scent. He shook his head and carried on.

"We need to find him. He's been missing now for a day and a night," said Pickle.

"I think Timmy has kidnapped him," said Pogo Paws.

"Why would he do that?" asked Lennie.

"Zip it, Lennie!" sighed Pickle and Pogo

Badger the Mystical Mutt

Paws together.

"Right, we need to arm ourselves. This could be war," snarled Pogo Paws.

"Yes, dogs against cats. Let's settle this once and for all," growled Pickle.

"Oh, are we dressing up?" asked Lennie excitedly.

Pogo Paws and Pickle looked at Lennie in despair, before they all headed off to the bins to see what they could find.

In the shed, Timmy and Snif shared a few slices of cold toast.

"I'm so sorry about the way I've been treating you, Timmy. How can I ever thank you for saving my life yesterday?" asked Snif.

"I'm sure you would have done exactly the same, if you'd been in my position," said Timmy modestly.

Snif shrugged and said, "I suppose we don't know how we'll react until we're in that situation, but I know how much cats hate water."

"It's not exactly my *favourite* place to be, especially not freezing cold water, but I didn't have any choice."

"Well, I feel like doing something to show the others that cats and dogs can be pals," said Snif firmly.

"Can't we just *be* pals?" said Timmy.

"But you are such a hero, and you lost your badge too. I think it's important that everyone knows about your bravery. It's time to banish the age-old myth that dogs and cats loathe each other."

"What about the rest of the gang?" asked Timmy.

"Them?" snorted Snif. "I don't know why you wanted to be part of us? I'm ashamed to have been their leader."

"Aren't you still their leader?"

"No. As of this moment, I resign," said Snif decisively.

In the lane, Pogo Paws, Pickle and Lennie had donned their armour and chosen their weapons. They soon picked up Snif's scent and headed straight for the shed in Badger's garden.

Meanwhile, Badger was making his way to the duck pond. When he arrived, Badger held his neckerchief in his paw and addressed it solemnly.

"It's going to be dark, it's going to be wet, and it's going to be freezing, but I'm afraid I have to ask this of you, 'Chief."

He laid his neckerchief on the ice and said: *"'Chief, 'Chief, dive down deep, and fetch Timmy's collar back to keep."*

'Chief flew across the ice and plunged into the deep black hole.

Snuggled up in the shed, Snif was still thinking about what to do to bring cats and dogs together.

"If you're really serious, Snif, then we could set up some kind of place, where both cats and dogs could go, to maybe get some food and find some company if they're a bit lonely," suggested Timmy.

"Perfect. Like a drop-in centre?" said Snif excitedly.

Just then, Badger returned from his business with 'Chief.

"Brrrr!" said Badger shivering. "I need to dry out my neckerchief."

He hung his beloved neckerchief over a hook on the back of the door.

"There," said Badger throwing Timmy his collar. "That's all we could find, I'm afraid. Your badge is long gone."

"Thanks, Badger, and thank you, 'Chief, for trying. Never mind, at least I've got my collar back," said Timmy gratefully.

Suddenly, the door was booted open and there stood three warriors ready for battle.

Pogo Paws had a big silver sieve on his head, and raised a rolling pin high. Pickle held out a black bin lid as a shield, and had an old dishcloth tied around her head. Lennie was wearing a plant pot as a hat and was wrapped in shiny tinfoil.

"Raaaaaaaaaaaaaaaaaaaaaaaaaaaaaaaaaaa hh!" they roared. "We've come to save you, Snif."

Badger, Timmy and Snif stopped their cheerful chat and looked up in amazement.

"Save him from what?" asked Badger.

"So, Snif," spat Pickle, "you've not been in danger at all? You've just been busy, cosying up with your new best friends?"

"After all we've done for you, this is how you repay us?" snarled Pogo Paws.

"I've been terribly worried about you," added Lennie.

"Zip it, Lennie!" said Pickle and Pogo Paws together.

Suddenly, Pogo Paws charged towards Badger, Timmy and Snif, brandishing his rolling pin.

Chapter Twelve

Snif stood up tall and placed himself between the rolling pin and Badger and Timmy.

"Drop it now and step away from the rolling pin," barked Snif.

Pogo Paws laid down his weapon and backed off. Pickle kept hold of her bin lid shield, and Lennie began to peel off his tinfoil.

"Yes, this is where I've been. And if you knew anything at all, you would know why. While you were so busy trying to destroy Timmy yesterday, *he* was busy trying to save my life," continued Snif.

Pogo Paws and Pickle looked at each other, not quite sure what to say. Lennie, who was lurking at the back, simply said, "Nice one, Timmy."

"In fact, now is probably a good time to tell you, I'm not your leader any more. You're on your own. I resign."

A month later, when the bitter frost had become less bitter, Badger was on his way to see Timmy and Snif.

Ahead of him in the lane, he spied Pickle, Pogo Paws and Lennie. Pickle threw a scrunched-up paper ball behind her before running on with the others. Badger tutted at Pickle's littering, and stopped to pick it up.

He smoothed out the paper ball and read aloud:

"Today, you are cordially invited to the Grand Opening of PLOPP, the new local drop-in centre for *The Peaceful Living Organisation for Pooches and Pussycats*"

He smoothed it out some more.

"No more crumpledness here," he thought, as he marched on proudly to attend the opening of Timmy and Snif's new centre. He wanted to present Timmy with a very special gift.

Badger smiled as he walked past the easels with tail-wagging diagrams and signs for workshops explaining the body language of cats and dogs. He chuckled at one blackboard as he read the words: *Fundamental Difference No. 1. Dogs like to be liked; cats aren't bothered.*

And he giggled when he saw a group of dogs giving some cats a lesson on how to endear themselves to the Big Folk.

He passed a production line with recycled  cans of Buddy Bites and saw Snif in an apron with a net on his head, packing a thick yellow sludge into the cans.

"Hi, Badger," shouted Snif. "I'm chief-chunker. What do you think? It's our new papaya and pineapple preserve; perfect for preventing allergies caused by pet dander."

"Wow, that's amazing!" said Badger.

"We've just done a deal to supply the local lanes, and it's really catching on. We plan to expand across the duck pond soon, and we're doing a roaring trade on p-bay."

"Toastastic! Is Timmy here today?" he asked.

"Yes, he's over there," said Snif happily. "And his sneezes are long gone. This papaya and pineapple preserve sorted his allergy in a jiff of a jiffy."

Timmy was hosting a session to his fellow cats on, "Conquering your fear of water", when Badger appeared shyly at his side.

"I just wanted to give you this, Timmy," said Badger holding out his paws.

Timmy looked and saw a shiny new Badger badge.

"But I thought ..." he gasped," that a Badger badge was a once-in-a-lifetime award, and I've already had mine"

"Yes, but you lost it during a remarkable feat of bravery, so I had another one made, just like it."

Timmy pinned it proudly to his collar and thanked Badger. Snif appeared by his side and pointed happily to the sign above the entrance.

"What do you think of our logo?" he asked.

Badger looked at the PLOPP lettering, which had a sprig of mistletoe entwined around it.

"I think it's very appropriate, Snif, as mistletoe is, after all, a symbol of peace and harmony. I wish you well with this. It's a really good thing you're doing for us all."

Snif and Timmy linked paws and smiled.

Out in the lane, Pogo Paws and Pickle were figuring out which of them would be leader. Neither of them had included Lennie in the vote.

"Why don't we do one potato, two potato?" suggested Lennie. "That seems the fairest way."

"Potato what?" said Pickle.

Lennie placed his paw in the centre of them, and said "One potato", then invited Pickle to put her paw on top and say, "two potato".

Pogo Paws joined in, and as he placed his paw on top of Pickle's paw, he said "three potato".

Lennie used his other paw to put on top of the pile of paws and said "four". He pointed to Pickle to use her other paw.

"Five potato?" Then Pogo Paws made "six potato", and Lennie "seven potato".

Pickle looked at Lennie as she had no paws left.

"Right," sighed Lennie. "Here's how it works: one potato, two potato, three potato, four; five potato, six potato, seven potato, more. We just keep putting our paws in, and when you've used up one, you put it behind your back. The first to have no paws left at the end is 'it'."

"What do you mean 'it?'" asked Pickle.

"The new gang leader, of course," said Lennie, pretty sure that he'd counted it out *not* to be him.

"I get it, I get it," said Pickle excitedly. "This is a good game. Right, I'll start it off."

Pickle did her "one potato". Lennie followed with "two potato", and Pogo Paws with "three potato". And so they continued with, "four, five potatoes, six potatoes, seven potatoes, more", and soon they each had one paw behind their back.

Then they carried on with the next round.

Lennie crossed his eyes and hoped he'd counted properly, with his one remaining paw still in the game.

But he hadn't.

As he placed his other paw behind his back, Pogo Paws and Pickle looked at him in astonishment.

"You're 'it'. You're actually 'it'. You're our new gang leader," they shouted together in horror.

"Looks like I am," grinned Lennie,

wondering just how on earth he was going to cope with the responsibility.

Badger trotted back to his garden feeling very pleased with himself.

"Another Badgical-Magical job well done," he thought.

Then he saw it, glinting next to the sundial.

His treasured Wim-Wim had returned.

It clanked and rattled to greet him. He took off his neckerchief and polished its reverse plunger lovingly.

The Wim-Wim was back and ready for the next Badgical-Magical adventure.

ALSO PUBLISHED BY THE LUNICORN PRESS

Badger the Mystical Mutt
ISBN: 978-0-9569640-0

**Badger the Mystical Mutt
and the Barking Boogie**
ISBN: 978-0-9560640-1-4

www.badgerthemysticalmutt.com